HAMBONE

Why Pigs Have Curly Tails

Illustrations, interior and cover design by Design Art Studio
www.designartstudio.net

Published by

Halifax, NS
info@ocpublishing.ca
www.ocpublishing.ca

ISBN - 978-1-989833-02-5 (Paperback Edition)

ISBN - 978-1-989833-03-2 (Hard Cover Edition)

**Dedicated to my children Trish and Barbara
and grandchildren Emma and Andrew**

Long, long ago, when the world was very young, there was a little pig named Hambone.

Hambone lived at Farmer Brown's farm with his mother Porcina, his brother Rufus, and his sister Prunella. They all enjoyed playing with the dogs and cows and donkeys and loved the treats Farmer Brown provided—like corn cobs and vegetable scraps. The whole family loved to wallow in the puddles in their sty because getting all covered with mud was just what pigs do.

Just like all the other pigs, Hambone was round and pink with a long, straight tail. Yes, all pigs had long, straight tails in those days.

Hambone looked like all the other pigs but he was different.

Hambone was different because he had very unusual tastes . . . he so desperately wanted a DILL PICKLE! Now, how did Hambone know about dill pickles? Well, he had seen Farmer Brown chomping on something green and drippy . . . something that made Hambone's mouth water.

"Momma?" Hambone asked. "What is that green thing Farmer Brown is eating? It's making my mouth all watery."

"That's a dill pickle," said Porcina Pig. "They are a delicacy enjoyed by humans but I don't know why, because they are green and drippy and sour."

Hambone hungered for that wonderful, sour, mouth-watering smell.

Hambone decided that he didn't want just any old dill pickle.

Hambone wanted the biggest, greenest, drippiest, crunchiest, sourest, most mouth-puckering dill pickle in the entire world.

Hambone thought and dreamed and thought and dreamed about that pickle night and day.

Finally, Hambone couldn't stand it any longer.

He decided to go out into the world and find that special pickle.

Hambone put on his new red and green plaid jacket with the three silver buttons.

He packed a knapsack with all his most precious things: seven bags of sunflower seeds, four rosy red apples, five coloured ribbons, a bottle of oink (which is just like ink only it is pink), and a new piggly pen to write with.

Then, brushing a tear from his little pink snout, he said good-bye to his mother. Porcina hugged Hambone and said, "Be safe my darling little piglet. Remember I love you to the cow's meadow and back." Then Porcina kissed Hambone on his little pink snout and waved good-bye as Hambone started down the road.

Hambone walked and walked and walked.

There was no one else on the road and Hambone felt all alone and a little scared.

Finally, when the sun was high, a big, blue and yellow parrot swooped down out of the bright, blue sky, landed in a cloud of dust, and waddled toward Hambone.

"Please sir . . . uh . . . ma'am. I need some help. Can you tell me the way to the dill pickle place?" Hambone looked pleadingly at the big parrot.

The parrot stared at Hambone with black beady eyes. It stuck out one claw and squawked, "Aawrrk—Polly wants a cracker."

"I'm sorry," said Hambone. "I don't have any crackers."

"Awrrk!" squawked the parrot and flapped its wings.

"But—but," stammered Hambone. "I have sunflower seeds. Do you like sunflower seeds?"

Hambone dug into his knapsack and held out the seven bags of sunflower seeds. "I sure hope you like sunflower seeds."

"Awrrk—Polly wants seeds," squawked the parrot. She grabbed the seeds and stuffed them all into her beak.

Polly flapped her wings, and as she flew over Hambone he heard her mumble through a mouthful of seeds, "Urn eft atta tore."

"I don't understand. What kind of direction is 'Urn eft atta tore'?" he called, but Polly the Parrot was gone.

Hambone sighed and continued down the hot, dusty road.

About two hours later, he sat down to rest in the shade of a great oak tree.

Just as he was opening his knapsack to get out a rosy red apple to munch on, he heard a crashing, thrashing noise behind him.

A roly-poly little man in a tall white hat flew out of the bushes in a cloud of flour and burst into tears.

"Oh—oh—woe is me. I'm ruined. I'm wrecked. Oh, woe is me," wailed the roly-poly little man.

"What's the matter?" asked Hambone. "Please stop crying. Maybe I can help."

"No one can help me," sobbed the roly-poly little man, wiping his nose on his sleeve. "The King will banish me—or put me in the dungeon. Oh—Oh—Oh!" The roly-poly little man burst into a new flood of tears.

"Why would the King do that?" asked Hambone.

"Because I promised to make him an apple dumpling, and now I can't find even one apple in all the land. Oh, woe is me!" cried the roly-poly little man.

"Oh," cried Hambone with glee. "I can help. Just look!"

He pulled the four rosy red apples from his knapsack and held them up in front of the roly-poly little man.

"If I give these to you, will you tell me the way to the dill pickle place, please?"

The roly-poly little man danced with joy. He grabbed the apples and kissed Hambone on his little pink snout.

"Thank you, little pig. You saved me. The King will be so pleased with me!" He spun in a happy circle, did a jig, and turned back to Hambone. "Follow this road over the hill and turn left at the store and there you are."

And the roly-poly little man ran off clutching the rosy red apples.

Hambone said, "You're welcome, I'm sure."

As he started up the hill, a surprised look came over his face. "Of course—that's what Polly the Parrot meant to say, 'Turn left at the store' not, 'Urn eft atta tore'."

Hambone hopped and skipped up the hill and whistled a happy tune.

Just over the top of the hill, Hambone thought he saw the store.

He turned left and walked on hopefully.

Hambone walked.

He skipped.

He ran.

He jogged and walked some more.

Finally, he came to a very wide river.

Hambone looked for a bridge to cross the river, but there was no bridge!

Poor Hambone! He stood right in the middle of the dusty road and cried. Hambone cried so much that his tears made a big mud puddle. He was just about to jump into the puddle and have a good wallow, because that's what you do when things don't go your way, when he heard a deep, gruff voice.

"What's wrong, little pig? Are you crying wee-wee-wee all the way home?"

Hambone looked up. There stood a gray and wrinkly elephant.

Hambone gulped back a sob and said, "Oh, Mr. Elephant. Can you please help me? I need to get across the river, but there's no bridge and I don't know what to do."

Hambone dripped tears onto his dusty little hooves.

"There, there, little pig," boomed the elephant. "Just you stop crying. Ellington Elephant will fix that."

Ellington slowly walked along the riverbank, pushing and tugging at each tree.

When he came to an enormously tall pine tree, he wrapped his trunk around it.

The big elephant pushed and pulled with all his mighty might.

The tree creaked and cracked.

Ellington grunted and groaned.

With a great snap! and splash! the tree fell across the river. It was almost like a real bridge!

"Oh, thank you so much Mr. Ellington Elephant," called Hambone as he ran to the tree bridge. "I'm really ever so grateful to you."

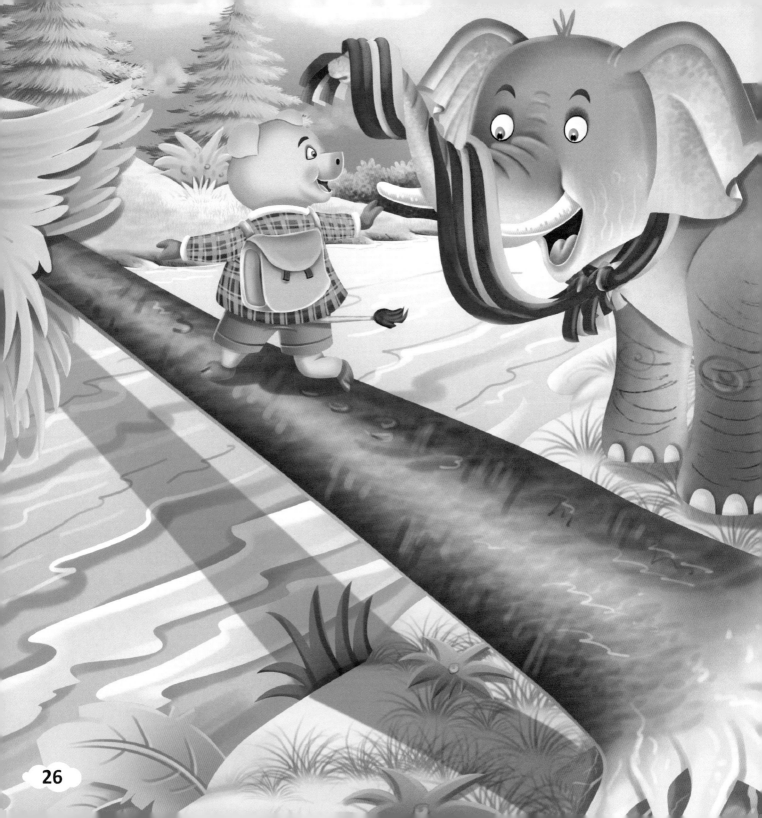

"Oh—oh!" Ellington cried. "By dose—id hurds! I thig id's brogen."

"Let me see," said Hambone, gently touching the elephant's great gray trunk. "No, it's not broken—just sprained."

Hambone reached into his knapsack and pulled out five coloured ribbons.

He tied the ribbons together, then carefully lifted the injured trunk into the sling.

"There," said Hambone. "Does that feel better?"

"Oh—id does. I'll be vine avder a sleeb."

Ellington flopped down with an earth-shaking thump.

Hambone patted the elephant on the leg. "Thanks again for making the bridge, Ellington Elephant. Good-bye." Then Hambone gingerly picked his way across the pine tree bridge.

On the other side of the river, Hambone stopped and took a deep breath.

Dill pickle smells filled his little pink snout!

His mouth started to water just like it had when he smelled Farmer Brown eating the juicy, drippy, sour green thing.

He ran and ran and finally he reached it—the dill pickle place!

Hambone knocked loudly on the door.

"What—what—who's there?" screeched a raspy voice. The door opened and a very, very, very old lady stood there.

She wore a dark green dress. Her hair was knotted on the top of her head. Her face was wrinkled and brown. She looked like a pickle!

"A pig!" she squeaked. "What do you want?"

Hambone gulped and stammered, "Please ma'am. I-I-I'd like a dill pickle."

The old woman cackled, "A dill pickle for a pig! What a silly thing that would be."

She peered down at Hambone. "And if I did have a dill pickle for you, little pig, what would you pay me for it?"

Hambone felt his heart drop. How could he pay for a pickle?

"I-I-I don't know," he stammered. "I didn't think to bring any money."

Sadly, he turned away, ears and tail drooping with disappointment.

"Wait," muttered the old woman, touched by Hambone's sadness. "Maybe we can make a trade. What have you got in that knapsack, little pig?"

Hambone turned slowly. "All I have left is a bottle of oink and a new piggly pen." He sighed loudly and his shoulders drooped.

"Hmmm—oink and a piggly pen, eh! Could you make me a sign with them?" asked the old woman.

"Oh, yes," cried Hambone eagerly. "I can make you a very fine sign with my bottle of oink and my new piggly pen."

"Well, then," said the old woman. "You make me a sign that says 'Dill Pickles for Sale' and I'll give you one pickle."

Hambone set to work, and in no time at all he made a beautiful sign complete with hearts and squiggles.

When he was done, he gave it to the old woman and she said, "Good. It's perfect! Now go pick out your pickle, little pig."

Hambone reached into the deepest barrel. He pulled out the biggest, greenest, drippiest, crunchiest, sourest, most mouth-watering dill pickle that ever there was!

Hambone closed his eyes.

He opened his mouth.

He took an ENORMOUS bite of dill pickle.

Oh! Oh! Oh! Hambone's ears stood straight up. His eyes watered. His mouth puckered.

And his long, straight piggy tail—well—it just curled right up—SPROING!

Hambone cried, "Whoops—what just happened?" as he tried to peer backwards at his tail.

The little, old lady laughed and laughed. She said, "I guess that green, drippy, crunchy, sour, mouth-watering pickle just curled your long, straight tail right up tight. And I think it might just always stay that way!"

So that is why, to this very day, little pigs have curly tails.

Praise from Educators

Praise from Educators

"*Hambone-Why Pigs Have Curly Tails*, tells a unique and exciting tale about perseverance, kindness, and a search for excitement in our lives."

Laura Shepherd, Literacy/Numeracy Specialist

"An utterly delightful book that captures the imagination and intrigue with animals, life on the farm, and adventures. Hambone is rich in vocabulary development with a storyline that is both enduring and layered in depth and lessons. Adults and children alike will come back to this book again and again. As a special learning support teacher and primary teacher, I am thrilled with the rich vocabulary. I would recommend this book to any library, teacher, parent, and speech and language pathologist."

Linda Whittle, Elementary and Special Learning Support Teacher

"A charming story and characters, very readable, enjoyable, light, and sweet. I love the onomatopoeia and alliteration, fun verbs; the use of language appeals to the senses and adds fun to the story. Kids will love the characters and descriptions of them, and the pickle as the object of obsession is funny. There is a mission, it's solved at the end, and kids love that. Reading with kids is an important, wonderful daily activity to share. You can connect with each other, make predictions about the plot, use imagination and visualize, improve language skills, and expand vocabulary. It's one of the most special rituals to have in daily family life."

Jane Kristoffy, Educational Strategist, Right Track Educational Services

"I think kids connect to unique and eccentric characters like Hambone. What kid wouldn't find delight and humour with a story about a pig on an adventure to get his first dill pickle but ends up with a curly tail?"

Kylie Etmanskie, Elementary School Teacher

"I absolutely loved reading this story aloud-and believe me, I read a LOT of books as a kindergarten teacher and mom! The choice of vocabulary and detailed storytelling not only made it fun to read, but it painted a clear picture in my mind as Hambone went on his adventure. This story is joyful and reminds us of the importance of being kind to others. Children and their grown-ups will share some giggles, and reflect on the importance of being kind, as they follow along on Hambone's adventure to find his juicy, mouth-watering treat!"

Kate Mays, Kindergarten Teacher

Hambone - Why Pigs have Curly Tails is much more than a tale of tails. In a Tech Age it is refreshing to see very human values given some space. This is definitely a book for shared reading; for thinking, talking, and exploring ideas. Because the text contains lines that are short and repetitive, a young child could even begin to share in the reading.

Hambone is a gentle book, giving a thoughtful reader the opportunity to raise many issues such as what it is like to be different; what it is like to have goals that are not shared by your community. It breaks easily into sections so it could be treated as a continued story. As Hambone confronts obstacles along the way, he does not resort to giving up on his dream or TANTRUMS! However, this story does not shy away from the possibility of tears.

The illustrations contribute much to the story. Hambone will be an Island of Calm in our Sea of Uncertainty."

Marilyn Stairs, Retired Elementary School Teacher

"*Hambone-Why Pigs Have Curly Tails* is a delightful story of Hambone's adventures as he searches for the perfect dill pickle! Along the way, Hambone demonstrates kindness in his many acts of giving, as he also learns about perseverance. The illustrations are perfect for this age group and the plot will easily keep children engaged."

Sheila Howlett, Library Technician

About the Author

Jackie Arnason is a prairie girl. She was born in a small town in Saskatchewan and spent most of her life in Regina, Saskatchewan.

While growing up in the "dirty thirties" life was hard. The library became her haven. She learned to love books of all kinds and made up stories to tell her brothers and sisters.

As an adult she married and had children and then grandchildren. Here at last was a captive audience, so she told stories about pigs and dragons and kittens and clouds and zebras. The stories fostered a closeness between mother and daughters and grandmother and grandchildren and had a gentle and imaginative way of teaching life lessons.

Despite the fact that she is now in her 80's, Jackie still loves to tell stories, using her imagination to bring joy to others. She is essentially a story teller, a mom, an Ahma, a mentor, a reader, a writer and a delighted first-time author. Learn more about Jackie at https://www.ocpublishing.ca/jackie-arnason.html